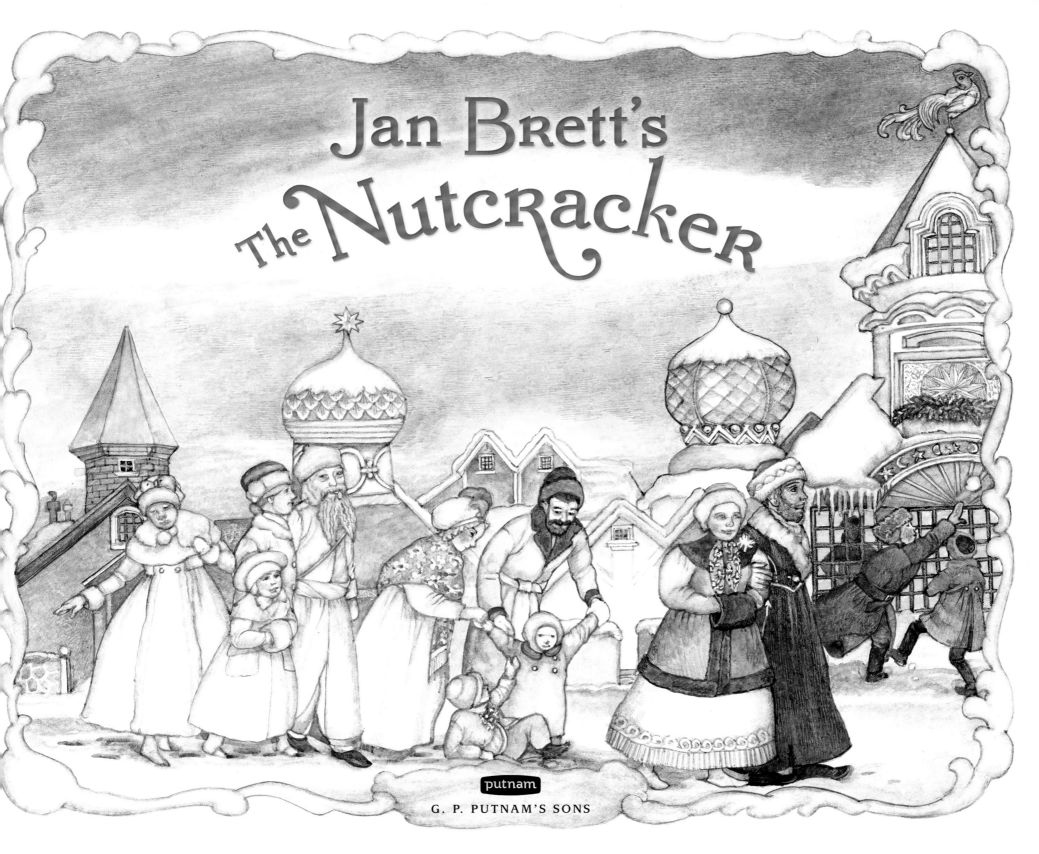

Jan Brett's The Nutcracker

putnam

G. P. PUTNAM'S SONS

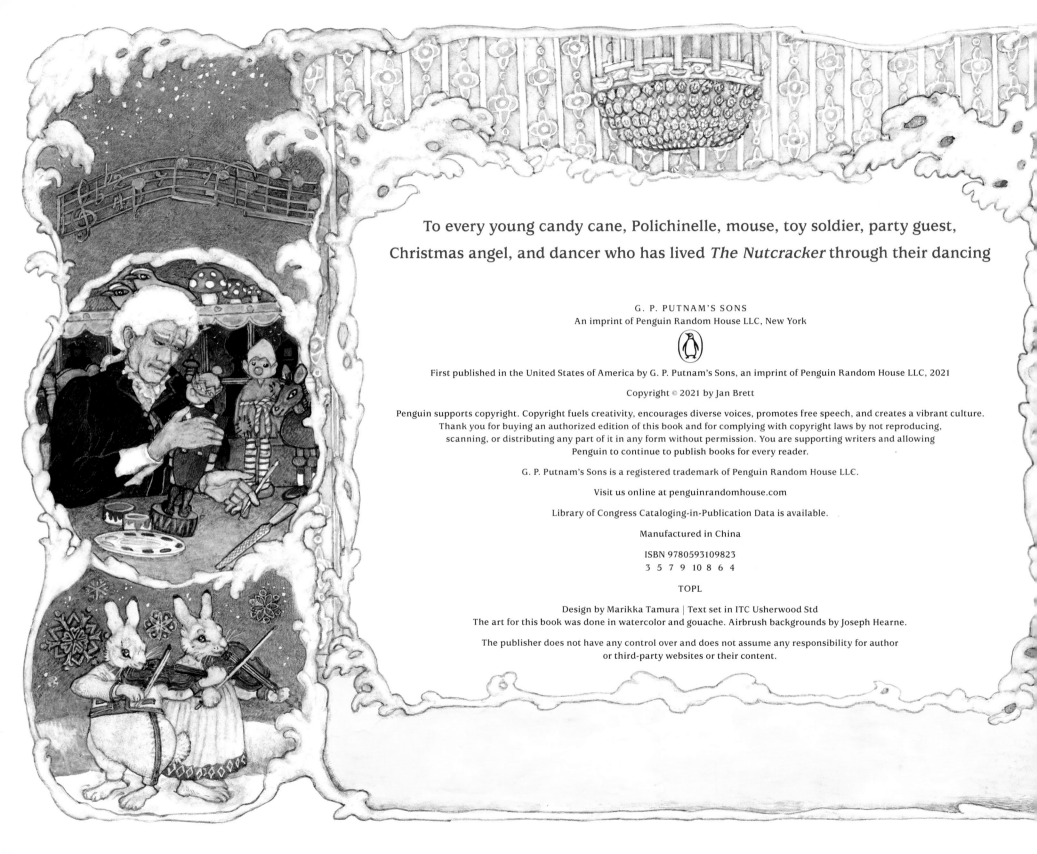

To every young candy cane, Polichinelle, mouse, toy soldier, party guest, Christmas angel, and dancer who has lived *The Nutcracker* through their dancing

G. P. PUTNAM'S SONS
An imprint of Penguin Random House LLC, New York

First published in the United States of America by G. P. Putnam's Sons, an imprint of Penguin Random House LLC, 2021

Visit us online at penguinrandomhouse.com

Library of Congress Cataloging-in-Publication Data is available.

Manufactured in China

ISBN 9780593109823
3 5 7 9 10 8 6 4

TOPL

Design by Marikka Tamura | Text set in ITC Usherwood Std
The art for this book was done in watercolor and gouache. Airbrush backgrounds by Joseph Hearne.

The publisher does not have any control over and does not assume any responsibility for author or third-party websites or their content.

"Sounds like Christmas, smells like Christmas, it *is* Christmas!" Marie laughed.

"Thumps and bumps and jingling bells—I'm ready!" whooped her brother, Fritz.

The doors opened into a magical Christmas party.
But Marie never could have guessed how magical. Not far away,
Uncle Drosselmeier was gathering the curious creations he had
fashioned for Christmas Eve.

Uncle Drosselmeier wheeled in the mysterious boxes. Inside were
a trickster and two harlequins. With a turn of his key, a *whirr-whirr*,
and a *hum-hum-hum*, they danced.

The figures were so lifelike, everyone wanted to join the fun and dance along.

But Marie was enthralled by the Nutcracker her uncle had placed under the tree. "He looks like a real boy," she mused, "who has traveled from a place far away."

The partygoers danced the grand march and the quadrille, and applauded the beautiful music.

Uncle Drosselmeier arrived at Marie's side. He placed a hazelnut in the Nutcracker's mouth. *Crack!* Out came a perfect nut.

Marie beamed. *What a surprising fellow he is,* she thought.

It was late when Marie's mother pleaded with
her to say good night to the guests, but Marie would
not leave the Nutcracker.

Fritz, wanting to see how he worked, had broken the Nutcracker, and Marie
was helping him get better.

When the house was silent, Marie lay awake in her bed. *I better check on the Nutcracker,* she thought.

She tiptoed past Uncle's old carved clock with the watchful owl on top.

In the eerie light, Marie felt odd. As the old clock chimed twelve, she
seemed to be getting smaller, or everything around her was growing bigger.
Strange sounds were coming from inside the walls.
Scritchy scratchy squeak, scritchy scratchy squeak.
Then Marie saw a mouse as bold as brass who wore a glittery crown.

Slowly, the old gilded cabinet holding Uncle's wonderful gifts from times past creaked open. The figures inside moved as if waking up, and Marie heard the sounds of mice gathering at her back. Fritz's toy soldiers were mustering forces.

Then a strong, clear voice called, "We will not stand for any
mouse invasion or their wicked king!"
It was the Nutcracker, now a boy, on his feet and on the move.

It was a ferocious battle. The Nutcracker jumped into the thick of it. *Crack!* The soldiers marched and the mice pounced. Then the Mouse King leaped upon the Nutcracker.

Brave Marie reached for her slipper, took exacting aim, and toppled the wicked Mouse King in one blow. The Nutcracker was saved!

The battle was won, and the wicked Mouse King was vanquished.
The soldiers formed a hero's arch for Marie and the Nutcracker.

At the end of the arch, Marie whispered, "What is this?" For inside
the cabinet, the door to the gingerbread house was open. A sleigh was waiting
for them, and Marie and the Nutcracker stepped in.

A wintry figure beckoned them forward as she danced among the snowflakes.

The sleigh glided through a dreamland of icicles until they heard lively music—molto vivace—playing. Dancing bears performed the Russian Trepak. All thoughts of the battle and the Mouse King disappeared as the music reached their ears, then their hearts, and down to their very toes.

They leaped higher and higher until the one with a twinkle in his eye
lifted Marie skyward before gently placing her into the sleigh.

Next they were gliding through a birch copse.

The wintry lady escorted them to a sparkling clearing where two elegant foxes performed the Danse Arabe, their foxtails entwining.

Marie, standing on her toes, imagined the handsome fox spinning her as part of the dance.

When the foxes bowed toward the lady and the Nutcracker applauded, Marie exclaimed, "She must be the princess of this snowy land!"

As the sleigh followed the Snow Princess, the treetops suddenly exploded. A large creature careened through them, sprinkling the woodland with dazzling snow crystals. The dragon's breath was harrumphing out in song: *humph-humph, humph-humph.*

With great fanfare, two flying squirrels leaped off its back
and invited Marie and the Nutcracker for a cup of tea from
their samovar.

As the sky grew the color of a sugar plum and the snow became many shades of blue, hundreds of tiny flames appeared, and lanterns illuminated the path. Antlered friends playing flutes led them toward a gingerbread house.

The Nutcracker smiled at Marie, his eyes happy and sad
at the same time, like the music.

"Are we heading back home already?" asked Marie.

"Not quite yet," whispered the Snow Princess.

They peeked through the gingerbread windows at bouquets of spring
flowers swooping and twirling to a waltz. But they also saw bustling prickles.
"I thought hedgehogs slept through the winter." Marie laughed.

"You just have to find their gingerbread palace to see them,"
answered the Nutcracker.

The Snow Princess smiled. "We have an even bigger treat ready for you."

The gingerbread doors opened. The animal orchestra performed the Waltz of the Flowers. Candy cane elves and fairies danced for the Nutcracker to celebrate his bravery in standing up to the wicked mice. Mother Ginger and her chicks thanked Marie for throwing the slipper that changed the course of the battle.

The celesta's twinkling notes and the whirling dancing made Marie's imagination take flight for what seemed like hours.

As her eyelids, and the Nutcracker's, grew heavy, the doors to the old cabinet creaked open and beckoned them back to Marie's home.

The next day, Marie was happy to wake up to her mother's loving face and Fritz's mischievous smile. Her Nutcracker was by her side, and almost everything was as before.

But from that day forward, even when she was grown, if she heard the notes of the celesta, she felt she and the Nutcracker were back in the land of the Snow Princess once more.